Billie
the Baby Goat
Fairy

Join the **Rainbow Magic Reading Challenge!**

Read the story and collect your fairy points to climb the

To Nancy, Nell and Peggy

Special thanks to
Rachel Elliot

First published in Great Britain in 2017 by The Watts Publishing Group

1 3 5 7 9 10 8 6 4 2

A CIP catalogue record for this book is available from the British Library.

ISBN 978 1 40834 518 4

Printed and bound in Great Britain by CPI Group (UK) Ltd, Croydon, CR0 4YY

The paper and board used in this book are made from wood from responsible sources.

Orchard Books
An imprint of Hachette Children's Group
Part of The Watts Publishing Group Limited
Carmelite House, 50 Victoria Embankment, London EC4Y 0DZ

An Hachette UK Company
www.hachette.co.uk
www.hachettechildrens.co.uk

Billie
the Baby Goat
Fairy

by Daisy Meadows

ORCHARD

www.rainbowmagic.co.uk

The Fairyland Palace

Farmhouse

Pond

Fluttering Fairyland Farm

Greenfields Farm

Greenfields House

Barn

Pond

Jack Frost's Spell

I want a farm that's just for me,
With animals I won't set free.
It's far too slow to seek each one.
Let fairy magic get this done!

With magic from the fairy farm,
I'll grant my wish – to their alarm!
And if I spoil the humans' fun,
Then Jack Frost really will have won!

Contents

A Big Day and a Big Problem

The sun was shining brightly on Greenfields Farm, and the fresh early-morning breeze made it the perfect spring day. Butterflies and bees were already busy around the flowers and bushes. Rachel Walker and her best friend Kirsty Tate were walking away from the farmhouse, feeling a very special kind of excitement.

"The big day has finally arrived," said Kirsty, pausing to take a long, deep breath of fresh country air. "I can't wait for the grand opening to start!"

The girls – together with Kirsty's parents – had been staying at the farm during spring half term to help the Tates' friends, Harriet and Niall Hawkins, get the farm ready to welcome visitors.

"I want to be sure that everything is perfect," said Rachel.

The girls had been given the very special job of looking after the baby farm animals. They had loved every minute of it, and this morning they had woken up extra early so that they could check on all the baby animals before the grand opening.

"Let's visit the ducklings first," said Kirsty.

They walked past the barn and along the winding path that led to the duck pond. As soon as they had walked between the trees, they saw the glittering water of the pond, with its tall reeds and its happy ducks. Lots of little ducklings were quacking as they splashed around.

"They all look fine," said Rachel. "Shall we check the lambs next? I love the way they bounce around when they see us. It's as if they've got springs in their hooves."

In the sheep pasture, the lambs bounced just as lambs should, and Rachel and Kirsty gave them some food and patted their fluffy white wool. Their eager baaing made the girls smile.

"Foals next," said Kirsty. "I wonder if

they will still be clean after the bath we
gave them yesterday?"

"No way," said Rachel, laughing. "You
know how much they love rolling in all
those muddy puddles."

Sure enough, when they arrived at the
stables, they found all the foals coated in
mud, neighing happily as they rolled and
splashed.

"I'm so glad they're all OK," said Kirsty. "Thank goodness Jack Frost and his pesky goblins haven't caused any more trouble."

"At least not yet," said Rachel.

On their first day at Greenfields Farm, Kirsty and Rachel had met the Baby Farm Animal Fairies and visited the Fluttering Fairyland Farm, a magical farm hovering in mid-air among the puffy white clouds. The Baby Farm Animal Fairies – Debbie the Duckling Fairy, Elodie the Lamb Fairy, Penelope the Foal Fairy and Billie the Baby Goat Fairy – showed the girls their magical baby farm animals, who lived at the farm.

But while the girls were visiting the rest of the animals with Francis the Fairyland Farmer, Jack Frost had stolen the magical baby farm animals Splashy the duckling, Fluffy the lamb, Frisky the foal and Chompy the baby goat.

"I keep thinking about poor Snowdrop and the snow goose," said Kirsty. "I hope they're getting a bit more love and attention from Jack Frost now."

Jack Frost had taken the animals because he wanted his own private petting farm at his Ice Castle. The snow goose and her baby, Snowdrop, were Jack Frost's pets, and they loved him to bits. But Jack had been so busy chasing after the magical baby farm animals that he had been neglecting the snow geese.

"Me too," said Rachel. "But most of all I'm thinking about Billie the Baby Goat Fairy. The fairies need *all* the magical baby farm animals to be safe, or they won't be able to look after baby farm animals everywhere. As long as Chompy is missing, the fairies can't look after the animals."

Over their last few days at Greenfields Farm, Rachel and Kirsty had seen baby farm animals doing some very strange things indeed. The ducklings had acted like puppies, the lambs had acted like kittens and the foals had acted like piglets. So far, the girls had managed to get three of the fairies' magical baby animals back from Jack Frost and his mischievous goblins. But Chompy the baby goat was still missing.

Rachel and Kirsty made their way to the fenced pen where the goats lived. Gilbert, the baby, was always waiting for them at the top of the humpback bridge. But today, something was wrong. The bridge was empty.

"Where is he?" asked Kirsty.

They hurried nearer, and then they saw the little goat. He wasn't prancing around like usual. He was pecking the ground and making a very strange sound indeed.

"It's almost like clucking," said Kirsty.

She and Rachel turned to each other as they realised what had happened.

"He thinks he's a chicken," said Rachel. "Jack Frost and his naughty goblins are still causing trouble."

"We have to find Chompy," said Kirsty, looking at her watch. "The farm opens in an hour. There's no time to lose!"

Panic in the Henhouse

Just then, Kirsty let out an excited little squeal.

"Rachel, look at that bucket of feed in the goat pen," she said.

It seemed to be an ordinary metal bucket, but Rachel trusted her best friend. She knew of only one thing that could make Kirsty sound so excited in the middle of a crisis. Fairy magic! She stared

at the bucket, and
then she saw
a little flare
of sparkling
light. It grew
brighter, until
the whole bucket
was glowing.
Then a tiny,
glittering fairy
shot out of the
bucket and high
into the air. She
whizzed around
like a firework, and then swooped down
to where the girls were standing.

"Hello, Rachel and Kirsty," she said,
a little out of breath. "It's me, Billie the
Baby Goat Fairy."

Billie was wearing blue dungarees with white spots and a T-shirt with floaty sleeves. Her eyes twinkled behind her glasses.

"Hello, Billie," said Rachel. "We're really glad to see you. Look at poor Gilbert — he thinks he's a chicken."

Billie fluttered down and perched on the top of the wooden fence. As soon as she saw Gilbert pecking the ground, she folded her arms and shook her head.

"I *must* get Chompy back home," she said. "I can't help any baby goats until we've found him. I came to tell you that one of the goblins has brought Chompy here to the farm. Will you help me search for him?"

"We're always glad to help our fairy friends," said Kirsty at once. "Where shall we look first?"

"It'll be easier to search the farm if we can fly over it and search for Chompy from above," said Rachel.

"Good thinking," said Billie, snapping her fingers. "No sooner said than done."

The girls ducked down behind the gate of the pen. They couldn't see anyone watching, but they didn't want to take any risks. Nobody else could find out about the fairies.

Billie waved her wand, and a flurry of
springtime flowers rose up and swirled
around the girls, hiding them from view.
Surrounded by the magical blooms,
Rachel and Kirsty felt themselves
shrinking to fairy size. Their hair was
sprinkled with petals as their fairy wings
grew. Then the flowers
fell to the ground
and the three
fairies fluttered
upwards
together.
From the
air, they
could see
the whole
farmyard laid
out like a map.

25

"There are the pigs, the sheep and the
horses," said Kirsty as they flew over
Greenfields Farm.

"No sign of the goblin or Chompy,"
said Kirsty. "There's Blossom the cow
beside the barn – we should check
inside."

They swooped into the barn, but it was
empty. Blossom let out a worried moo
and the fairies paused to pat her.

"Don't worry,
Blossom,"
Rachel
whispered in
her ear. "We're
trying to help
the farm."

Blossom nodded
her head in the direction of the chicken
coop behind the farmhouse. When the
fairies flew closer, they heard squawking,
flapping and alarmed clucking.

"Something is scaring the chickens,"
said Kirsty.

They zoomed across to the chicken
coop and landed beside the ramp that
led into the henhouse. A baby goat was
standing in the entrance, and the golden
glow of his coat told them who he was.

"Chompy!" said Billie.

Suddenly Chompy started moving down the ramp and the fairies saw that a goblin was trying to grab him. Chompy pushed back, and the goblin threw his arms around the baby goat's neck.

"Stop clucking," the goblin wailed. "I want a cuddle with you!"

But Chompy butted him and

disappeared. The squawking of the hens grew louder.

"Why is Chompy playing around the henhouse?" Rachel asked.

"Maybe he wants to sit on a nest like the hens," said Kirsty. "After all, he is acting like a chicken."

Suddenly an idea popped into Rachel's head.

"That's exactly what we need," she said. "A nest! Billie, can you make one big enough for Chompy to sit on?"

29

Billie waved her wand and a large nest appeared on the ground outside the henhouse.

"It's the perfect size for Chompy," said Rachel in delight. "Chompy, over here!"

Chompy scampered over and sat down on the big nest, clucking happily.

"Chompy,"

said Billie, fluttering towards him. He looked up at her and gave a confused little frown.

Rachel and Kirsty held hands and smiled. Any moment now, Chompy would be back to his normal self. But suddenly there was a loud crack of a bolt of icy blue magic, and then Jack Frost was standing in front of the nest.

Jack Frost's Shadows

Jack Frost dived for Chompy, but the magical baby goat lunged out of the nest and ran, squawking like a frightened chicken.

"Come back!" Jack Frost roared.

He raced after Chompy, and the fairies chased them both as fast as they could.

Rachel glanced back over her shoulder and saw a flurry of feathers as the goblin sat down among the chickens, wailing. Rachel felt almost sorry for him. Then she looked ahead again and saw Jack Frost charging after Chompy, yelling.

"They're going to cause chaos," Rachel said with a groan.

Harriet and Niall had spent the day before putting up signs and banners for the visitors. There were signposts to direct people to the pigs, the sheep, the horses and the goats, as well as the barn and the welcome centre. There were banners advertising tractor rides, donkey rides, bottle-feeding the baby farm animals, pig races and baby-animal cuddles. Hay bales had been dotted around for visitors to sit on.

But as Chompy hurtled across the farm, he wasn't looking where he was

going. All he cared about was getting
away from Jack Frost. He bumped into
the signs and knocked them down. He
ran at the banners with his head down,
ripping them and scattering them across
the farm. Jack Frost stampeded after him,
flinging hay bales out of his way to the
left and right.

The fairies fluttered overhead, feeling helpless. There was nothing they could do to stop the rampage.

"He's ruining everything," said Kirsty. "All the hard work we've been doing will be undone. If the visitors see the farm looking like this, they will never come back. We have to stop Jack Frost and save Chompy."

"I don't understand why Jack Frost is still so keen to steal baby animals for his petting farm," said Kirsty. "He's got his own baby goose, Snowdrop, back at his Ice Castle – and his snow goose, too. They love him. Why is he so greedy for more?"

"He is never happy with the things he's got," said Rachel. "Jack Frost always wants what other people have."

Just then, something caught her eye and she looked away from the chase. Two white shapes were following Jack Frost like shadows as he weaved across the farm.

"It's Snowdrop and her mother," said Kirsty. "They must have followed Jack Frost all the way from the Ice Castle."

"They really love Jack Frost," said Billie.

"They don't stop caring about him just because he's trying to find other animals."

"I've got an idea," said Kirsty. "We need to show Jack Frost what he's missing – and the snow geese can help us."

The three fairies hovered close together and Kirsty whispered her plan. Feeling hopeful, they all flew down to land in a field behind the barn. The snow geese were waddling towards them, a long way behind Jack Frost and Chompy.

Billie waved her wand, and a bowl of crisp green lettuce appeared beside the snow geese. They noticed it, and hurried over to nibble on the lettuce.

The fairies fluttered down beside them and spoke in soft voices.

"We want to talk to Jack Frost," said Kirsty. "Will you help us?"

The snow geese honked and nodded.

Gently, the fairies climbed on to the mother snow goose's back, scooping Snowdrop up with them.

"We'll follow Chompy and Jack Frost together," said Kirsty. "And when we reach them, we'll find a way to make Jack Frost see what wonderful pets he already has."

Ice Cold Heart

They soared into the sky and zoomed over the farm. It was delightful to be surrounded by the soft white feathers of the snow geese.

"It's like sitting inside a cloud," said Rachel, excitedly.

The farm was in a terrible mess, but the fairies were looking for just one thing – a little baby goat. At last they spotted him, and the snow goose changed direction. Chompy was in the goat pen, standing in the middle of the humpback bridge. Jack Frost had his arms around the little goat, and was cuddling him tightly and cackling with laughter.

"Stop struggling," Jack Frost was saying. "You're *my* pet now. You're going

to live in a lovely icy home. You'll like it.
Yes, you will."

Chompy wasn't listening. He was
wriggling, squawking and flapping his
legs as if they were wings. But Jack Frost
kept holding on, stopping him from
getting away.

The snow goose let out a sad little
honk and fluttered downwards, perching
on the railing of the bridge. The fairies
fluttered down to stand beside her, and
Jack Frost stared at them all in surprise.

"What are you doing here?" he
asked the snow goose. "And why are
you hanging around with those pesky
fairies?"

"They're allowed to have friends," said
Billie.

"Oh, no, they're not," Jack Frost

snapped. "They've got *me*. They don't need anyone else."

"Of course they are allowed to have other friends," said Billie. "And so is Chompy. He belongs at Fluttering Fairyland Farm with the other magical baby animals."

"You're not going to get him back,

ever," said Jack Frost. "He belongs with me now."

He cuddled Chompy even more tightly. Chompy gave a grumpy squawk.

"He doesn't belong with you," Rachel said. "He belongs with Billie. "He's not his true self without her."

"I'm taking Chompy to my petting farm at the Ice Castle," Jack Frost shouted. "That's where Snowdrop and the snow goose should be too. And once we're all there, no silly fairies are going to stop us."

The snow goose gave another miserable little honk, and Rachel looked into Jack Frost's cold eyes.

"Perhaps the snow goose and Snowdrop came to find you here because they've been missing you," said Rachel.

Kirsty saw the sad look on Snowdrop's face and nodded.

"Maybe they think that you don't love them any more," she said. "You've been so busy trying to get animals for your petting farm that you've stopped thinking about Snowdrop and the snow goose."

Chompy struggled again, dragging Jack Frost across the bridge.

"He doesn't *want* to be your pet," Kirsty called out. "But there are two animals here who *do* want to be with you."

Jack Frost stared at her, still clasping Chompy as tightly as he could. The snow goose nodded her long neck in agreement and Snowdrop fluttered up to sit on Jack's shoulder.

"The baby farm animals don't want to be part of your petting farm," Rachel said. "But the snow goose and Snowdrop truly love you."

The other fairies held their breath as they watched. Could the geese touch the Ice Lord's cold heart?

Jack Frost's Perfect Pets

Jack Frost looked at the snow goose,
who put her head on one side. Snowdrop
nuzzled his cheek with soft, white
feathers. Chompy was still pulling away
from him, but his snow geese were
longing to be with him.

Very slowly, Jack Frost loosened his
long, bony fingers from Chompy's wiry

hair. He took his arms away from
Chompy's neck. The little goat hurried

away, and Billie
fluttered over to
him. As soon
as she touched
him, he shrank
to fairy size
and bleated
happily.

"No more
chicken noises,"
said Rachel,
smiling. "He's
back to his normal self."

"Yes," said Billie. "And it's all thanks to
you, Rachel and Kirsty."

"You're welcome," said Kirsty. "We're
just happy that you have Chompy back."

Jack Frost patted little Snowdrop, who sat on his shoulder, and walked over to the snow goose. She lifted her head, and he stroked her gently. As Rachel and Kirsty watched, they saw his chin wobble. He sniffed, and then a tear rolled down his cheek.

"I'm so glad you love me," he said.

"Because I l-l-l…"

The fairies stared at the Ice Lord as he stammered.

"He's *really* not used to saying this word," said Kirsty.

Jack took a deep breath.

"I l-l-love you too," he said.

Rachel and Kirsty shared a smile.

"It's good to hear Jack Frost talking about happy feelings for a change," said Rachel.

"It's a truly happy ending," said Kirsty. "All except for the mess that Chompy and Jack Frost made on the farm. How are we going to explain it?"

"You won't have to," said Billie, tucking Chompy under her arm. "Follow me."

They all fluttered over Greenfields Farm and Billie waved her wand. Fairy dust was sprinkled across the farm. When it landed, the broken signs were instantly mended and the torn banners were repaired in a flash. The hay bales rolled back into position and all the stray bits of straw were cleared up.

"Are you going to take Chompy back to Fairyland now?" Rachel asked.

"Yes," said Billie. "Chompy and the rest of the magical baby animals are best looked after by Farmer Francis at

Fluttering Fairyland Farm."

"It's such a lovely place," said Kirsty. "I hope we can see it again some day."

"How about today?" Billie asked with a smile. "Would you like to come for another visit right now?"

"Yes, please!" Rachel and Kirsty said together.

The three fairies flew down to where Jack Frost was still cuddling his snow geese.

"You should come to Fluttering Fairyland Farm too," Billie said to Jack Frost. "I want to show you what a farm is like when the animals *want* to be there."

Jack Frost nodded, and Billie raised her wand. A sparkling flash of fairy dust whooshed around the little group, surrounding them with bands of light.

They were dazzled by it, and when the light faded, they blinked and gazed around in wonder. They were once more standing on the lush green grass of Fluttering Fairyland Farm. Farmer Francis was in front of them, and he smiled when he saw Jack Frost cuddling the snow geese.

"I see that Billie, Rachel and Kirsty have shown you that the pets you already have are special," said Francis.

Jack Frost had a real
smile on his face,
and everyone
could see that
for once, he
was feeling
truly happy.

"Your
animals are
nice," Jack Frost
said to Billie. "But my
snow geese are the best."

"That's exactly how you *should* feel
about your own pets," said Billie. "And
I'm glad you like ours too. But please
don't take them away from us again."

"You can visit the animals at the farm
whenever you want," said Farmer Francis.

"I would like that," said Jack Frost. "But

right now I am going to take my snow
goose and Snowdrop back home to the
Ice Castle."

The snow goose snuggled into him
and he stroked her feathers. He darted
a suspicious look around for a moment,
and then lowered his voice.

"I'm so sorry that I wasn't kind enough
to you both," he whispered. "I want to
make it up to you with lots of love and
cuddles."

The snow geese honked happily and
Jack Frost looked around again.

"Why is he looking so worried?" asked
Kirsty.

"I think he's checking that there are no
goblins around," said Rachel, laughing.
"He wouldn't want them to hear him
being so nice."

Farmer Francis turned to her and smiled.

"You and Kirsty are always welcome visitors too," he said. "There are four animals here who will always be grateful to you."

He stepped aside, and the girls saw the other three Baby Farm Animal Fairies, together with their magical

baby animals. The fairies flew over to
hug Rachel and Kirsty, and the animals
gathered in too, all happily back to their
normal selves.

"Thank you again, for everything,"
said Billie. "We wouldn't be here without
you."

Rachel and Kirsty gave each of the
magical animals a cuddle. Then, as
the fairies waved goodbye, Billie raised
her wand. In a blink the girls found
themselves standing beside the goat pen.
They were back on Greenfields Farm.

Open for Visitors

Gilbert was exactly where he belonged – standing by the humpback bridge and bleating.

"He's back to normal," said Kirsty.

"And at last all the baby farm animals are themselves again," said Rachel. "Thank goodness."

They shared a
happy glance as
Harriet appeared
around the side of
the farmhouse. She
waved at them.

"The official
opening is about to
start," she called. "Come
on – you mustn't miss it after all your
hard work."

Rachel and Kirsty raced across the
farm to join her. Niall was waiting for
them at the front of the farmhouse,
together with Kirsty's parents. They all
walked down to the main entrance gate,
sharing a lovely feeling of excitement.

"This is going to be a wonderful day,"
said Rachel happily.

"I hope we've thought of everything," said Harriet.

Niall squeezed her hand and smiled.

"The visitors will love it," said Mrs Tate in a confident voice. "You have turned Greenfields Farm into the perfect family day out."

There were lots of people at the main gate, and a red ribbon had been hung across the entrance. At the front of the crowd were two girls who looked about the same age as Rachel and Kirsty.

"Those girls are Emily and Isabel," said Niall. "They won our competition to officially open the farm and be the first ever visitors. Rachel and Kirsty, after the ceremony, will you show them around?"

Rachel and Kirsty nodded at once. They always loved the chance to make new friends.

"Emily and Isabel look really nice," said Kirsty. "I can't wait to show them all the sweet baby animals."

Niall and Harriet greeted the visitors and gave Emily and Isabel a special pair of enormous golden scissors.

"They make me feel as if we've shrunk to fairy size again," Rachel whispered, smiling at her best friend.

Emily used the scissors to cut the red ribbon.

"We now declare Greenfields Farm open for visitors," Isabel announced.

The crowd clapped and cheered, and then Harriet brought Emily and Isabel over to meet the girls.

"Rachel and Kirsty will show you around the farm," she said. "I hope you have a wonderful day."

Rachel and Kirsty linked arms with Emily and Isabel, and together they walked up towards the animals.

"What would you like to see first?"

Rachel asked.

"The lambs," said Emily.

"The ducklings," said Isabel.

The girls laughed, sharing the excitement of their new friends. Soon they were running around the farm together, hurrying from baby animal to baby animal, until Emily and Isabel had seen almost every single one.

"Just Gilbert left to visit," said Kirsty at last. "And we know where he'll be."

Sure enough, when they reached the goat pen, Gilbert was standing on the humpback bridge.

When he saw Rachel and Kirsty, he
let out a happy bleat and clomped
down from the bridge. There was a big
crowd of people watching him, and they
cheered and smiled when they saw how
much Gilbert loved his visitors. Laughing,
the girls petted him, but Emily and Isabel
hung back.

"Don't be afraid," said Rachel, looking
up at them. "He's really sweet. He might
try to nibble your clothes, but he won't
hurt you."

Emily and Isabel stepped closer. At
first they were nervous, but after a few
moments they realised how gentle the
baby goat was. Soon all four girls were
petting Gilbert, and he was delighted.

"He's gorgeous," said Emily.

Kirsty waved to her parents in the

crowd, and smiled as they came towards her with Harriet and Niall Hawkins.

"We want to thank you both for all your help getting the farm ready," Niall said. "Thanks to you, all our baby animals have been well cared for while we've been so busy. The open day is going brilliantly. Everyone seems to be having a great time."

"It's been hard work," Harriet added. "But it's all worth it now we can see how much the visitors are enjoying our farm."

"Our hard work was worth it, too," Rachel whispered into her best friend's ear.

"And lots of fun as well," Kirsty whispered back.

Niall and Harriet looked happy and relaxed now that everything was going so well. Rachel and Kirsty felt relaxed too, knowing that Jack Frost would be causing no more trouble for the Baby Farm Animal Fairies.

"I wonder when we'll have our next adventure with our fairy friends," said Rachel.

"Right now, I want to have an adventure with our new *human* friends," said Kirsty, grinning at Emily and Isabel. "An adventure exploring Greenfields Farm. Let's go!"

The End

Now it's time for Kirsty and
Rachel to help...

Kat the Jungle Fairy

Read on for a sneak peek...

"Here we are at last, boys and girls,"
said Mrs Hauxwell over the coach's
microphone. "Welcome to Jungle World."

Rachel Walker and her schoolfriends
gazed at the entrance to Jungle World
with their noses pressed against the coach
windows.

"It took a long time to get here from
Tippington School," said Mila, who was
sitting in the seat beside Rachel.

"It was worth it," said Rachel with a
grin. "This is going to be the best day
ever."

Not only was Jungle World an amazing

theme park and zoo, but Rachel's best friend, Kirsty Tate, was meeting her there. Both their schools were there to celebrate the end of term. They had been doing projects about the jungle for weeks.

"Mum arranged it all with Mrs Hauxwell," said Rachel. "I'm going to go round Jungle World with Kirsty's school group, so we can spend the day together."

"That's brilliant," said Mila. "You must miss her. I expect it's really hard that your best friend goes to a different school."

"Our adventures together make up for it," said Rachel with a little smile.

She and Kirsty shared a secret that had made their friendship even better. They were friends with the fairies. When they were together, magical adventures always seemed to be just around the corner.

Mila smiled back at her. She was a tall

girl with long hair and dark eyes that twinkled beneath a swishy fringe. As the coach stopped, Rachel noticed Mila's pink nail varnish and grinned. Nail varnish wasn't usually allowed at school, but the rules were different on the last day of term.

Read **Kat the Jungle Fairy** to find out what adventures are in store for Kirsty and Rachel!

Competition!

The Baby Animal Farm Fairies have created
a special competition just for you!

Collect all four books in the Baby Animal Farm series
and answer the special questions in the back of each one.

The Lamb Fairy is called

_ _ _ _ _

Once you have all four answers, take the first letter from
each one and arrange them to spell a secret word!
When you have the answer, go online and enter!

We will put all the correct entries into a draw and select
a winner to receive a special Rainbow Magic Goody Bag
featuring lots of treats for you and your fairy friends.
The winner will also feature in a new Rainbow Magic story!

Enter online now at www.rainbowmagicbooks.co.uk

Calling all parents, carers and teachers!
The Rainbow Magic fairies are here to help
your child enter the magical world of reading.
Whatever reading stage they are at, there's
a Rainbow Magic book for everyone!
Here is Lydia the Reading Fairy's guide to
supporting your child's journey at all levels.

Starting Out

Our Rainbow Magic Beginner Readers are perfect for first-time readers who are just beginning to develop reading skills and confidence. Approved by teachers, they contain a full range of educational levelling, as well as lively full-colour illustrations.

1

Developing Readers

Rainbow Magic Early Readers contain longer stories and wider vocabulary for building stamina and growing confidence. These are adaptations of our most popular Rainbow Magic stories, specially developed for younger readers in conjunction with an Early Years reading consultant, with full-colour illustrations.

2

Going Solo

The Rainbow Magic chapter books – a mixture of series and one-off specials – contain accessible writing to encourage your child to venture into reading independently. These highly collectible and much-loved magical stories inspire a love of reading to last a lifetime.

3

www.rainbowmagicbooks.co.uk

"Rainbow Magic got my daughter reading chapter books. Great sparkly covers, cute fairies and traditional stories full of magic that she found impossible to put down" - Mother of Edie (6 years)

"Florence LOVES the Rainbow Magic books. She really enjoys reading now" - Mother of Florence (6 years)

The Rainbow Magic Reading Challenge

Well done, fairy friend – you have completed the book!
This book was worth 5 points.

See how far you have climbed on the
Reading Rainbow opposite.

The more books you read, the more points you will get,
and the closer you will be to becoming a Fairy Princess!

How to get your Reading Rainbow
1. Cut out the coin below
2. Go to the Rainbow Magic website
3. Download and print out your poster
4. Add your coin and climb up the Reading Rainbow!

There's all this and lots more at
www.rainbowmagicbooks.co.uk

You'll find activities, competitions, stories, a special
newsletter and complete profiles of all the
Rainbow Magic fairies. Find a fairy with your name!